Oliver saves Christmas

By Vanessa Porkins

Little Oliver peered outside as it was just starting to snow,

What a shock he had when he saw a magical glow,

Santa and his reindeers had come down with quite a thump,

Poor Blitzen had picked up one almighty bump

Oliver walked towards the sled and saw this unruly sight,

Poor Santa had a terrible cold and looked up high with fright,

Without Blitzen on his team he might not complete his job,

And this got too much for Santa as he started then to sob,

Being the 24th December or Christmas Eve
as it's known,

There's very little time left for the presents
to be flown,

Oliver invited sad Santa and the reindeers
inside of his front door,

They sat down all thoughtful but got no further
than before,

After some tea and cake Oliver came up
with a plan,

He told each one of them and then
it all began,

Santa dosed up on cold medication with
reindeers all in line,

Blitzen was to have the night off and
all would be just fine

Replacing Blitzen on Santa's team was
Oliver and his Teddy,

They added extra power to the sled when all
were so ready,

Teddy was not an ordinary toy as it flew
up in the sky,

As Blitzen's powered lead made Teddy all magic
and able to fly,

This wonderful team with Oliver ,Teddy
Santa and Reindeers all,

Took right off and was to deliver such
a marvellous haul,

To Australia, China and Japan and everywhere
in between,

This partially Teddy driven sleigh was so fast
it was never seen,

It whooshed to here and whooshed to there,

Delivering down chimneys and up and down every stair,

Santa naturally did most of the delivering of gifts,

But to speed up he used Oliver to take presents up lifts,

As the night went on more places
were gifts delivered,

To warm places like Egypt and to Canada
where everyone shivered,

Not a single boy or girl was to be missed
off the list,

Except Oliver himself however that's where
there's a twist!

When the team of the night finally completed this task,

They realised they had very little time left to bask,

Santa was ever so grateful to Oliver as well,

But to wipe his night's memory Santa used a memory spell,

As Oliver awoke it was now Christmas day,

With no memory of last night's exertions
he wanted to play,

All excited he went down to see if
Santa had been,

And there was the most amazing gift that
he had EVER seen!

What was the gift I do hear you ask
what it could be?

Well wait till Christmas morning and
check under that tree,

I'm sure after all your wishes and
dreams will be met,

Here's wishing you the best Christmas yet!

MERRY CHRISTMAS

P.S. Thanks for Helping Santa this year
- I think Teddy still remembers helping.